D0923021

DATE DUE FEB 06

OCT 18 06			
GAYLORD			PRINTED IN U.S.A.

WITHDRAWN
Damaged, Obsolete, or Surplus

Jackson County Library Services

Bottled Sunshine

WITHDRAWN
Damaged, Obsolete, or Surplus

Jackson County Library Services

For my mother, who taught me to make jam
—Andrea

For Linda, Molly & Shadow of Udora and D & J of the Perfect Cottage
—Ruth

Text copyright © 2005 by Andrea Spalding
Illustrations copyright © 2005 by Ruth Ohi

Published in Canada by Fitzhenry & Whiteside, 195 Allstate Parkway, Markham, Ontario L3R 4T8
Published in the United States by Fitzhenry & Whiteside, 121 Harvard Avenue, Suite 2, Allston, Massachusetts 02134

All rights reserved. No part of this book may be reproduced in any manner without the express written consent of the publisher, except in the case of brief excerpts in critical reviews and articles. All inquiries should be addressed to Fitzhenry & Whiteside Limited, 195 Allstate Parkway, Markham, Ontario L3R 4T8.

www.fitzhenry.ca godwit@fitzhenry.ca

10 9 8 7 6 5 4 3 2 1
Library and Archives Canada Cataloguing in Publication
Spalding, Andrea
Bottled sunshine / Andrea Spalding; illustrations by Ruth Ohi.
ISBN 1-55041-703-7
1. Grandmothers—Death—Juvenile fiction. 2. Bereavement—Juvenile fiction. I. Ohi, Ruth II. Title.
PS8587.P213B68 2005   jC813'.54   C2004-906852-0

U.S. Publisher Cataloguing-in-Publication Data
(Library of Congress Standards)
Spalding, Andrea.
Bottled sunshine / Andrea Spalding ; illustrations by Ruth Ohi.
[32] p.: col. ill. ;cm.
Summary: Sammy learns to make blackberry jam during his last visit with his fun-loving grandmother, and the vivid memories of their time together sustain him after she passes away.
ISBN 1-55041-703-7
1. Grandmother and child – Fiction. 2. Death – fiction. I. Ohi, Ruth. II. Title.
[E] 22   PZ7.S7319Bo 2005

Fitzhenry & Whiteside acknowledges with thanks the Canada Council for the Arts, the Government of Canada through the Book Publishing Industry Development Program (BPIDP), and the Ontario Arts Council for their support of our publishing program.

Design by Christine Toller
Printed and bound in Hong Kong

Bottled Sunshine

Story by Andrea Spalding

Illustrations by Ruth Ohi

Fitzhenry & Whiteside

JACKSON COUNTY LIBRARY SERVICES
MEDFORD, OREGON 97501

The day was full of sunshine—everything sparkled.

 The tear on Sammy's cheek sparkled like a diamond.

 Sammy sniffed, then wiped his nose crossly. It was silly to be upset. Holidays had to end sometime.

 "Sammy, Sammy!" Grandma called from the cove. Sammy waved.

 "Phew! I'm not as young as I was," panted Grandma as she reached Sammy's rock. "But it's nice to sit here again. This was my favorite perch when I was your age."

Sammy eyed Grandma's wrinkles. It was hard to imagine her as a kid, but she must have been. She knew all about the secret caves, the deepest tide pools, and the best places to fish.

"Saying goodbye to your favorite places?" asked Grandma as she slipped an arm around his shoulder.

Sammy nodded sadly.

"Then it's time to bottle some sunshine to take back with you."

"Bottle sunshine?" exclaimed Sammy. "How do we do that?"

Grandma smiled. "Come with me."

They pulled on old tee-shirts and found baskets.

"You start," said Grandma. "Choose the sunniest blackberry patch on the island."

Sammy and Grandma walked along the lanes. Sammy looked in all the hedges. There were many blackberry patches but none seemed sunny enough.

They climbed a steep hill. "Stop!" said Sammy.

The sun was hot. It beat down on a tangle of brambles and glinted from a billion berries.

Sammy pointed. "That's got to be the sunniest blackberry patch on the whole island."

Grandma smiled. "Then we'll pick the berries and bottle their sunshine."

Grandma stepped up to the nearest bramble spray and started picking.

Sammy looked uneasily at the bush. "Too many bees."

"Bees are part of bottled sunshine," explained Grandma. "Listen to them hum. They pollinate the flowers so there are lots of blackberries each year."

Sammy watched the bees poking around the bushes. They ignored him. The buzz became a comforting song as he worked.

Grandma's nimble fingers flew in and out of the blackberry sprays, and the bottom of her basket was soon covered with juicy berries.

Sammy tried to copy her swift movements. "Ow!" He sucked his fingers. "Too many prickles."

"Prickles are part of it," explained Grandma. "They are the bushes' way of protecting the berries from the birds. Prickles help save the juiciest berries for you."

Sammy looked at the bushes. It was true. The biggest and the best berries were always surrounded by thorny sprays. He carefully lifted them aside and popped the plump juicy fruit in his basket and his mouth!

"BOO!" said Grandma. Her lips were berry-stained.

Sammy laughed. "Grandma," he crowed. "You look just like a blackberry."

Grandma laughed. "So do you, but I'm an old and wrinkled berry and you're a young one, plump with juice!"

Sammy snatched a gigantic berry from the middle of the bush. He leaned forward and popped it in Grandma's mouth. "Here's some juice to plump you up."

"Ummm," said Grandma, "I can feel it working."

"Is the juice part of bottled sunshine?" asked Sammy.

"The very best part," replied Grandma.

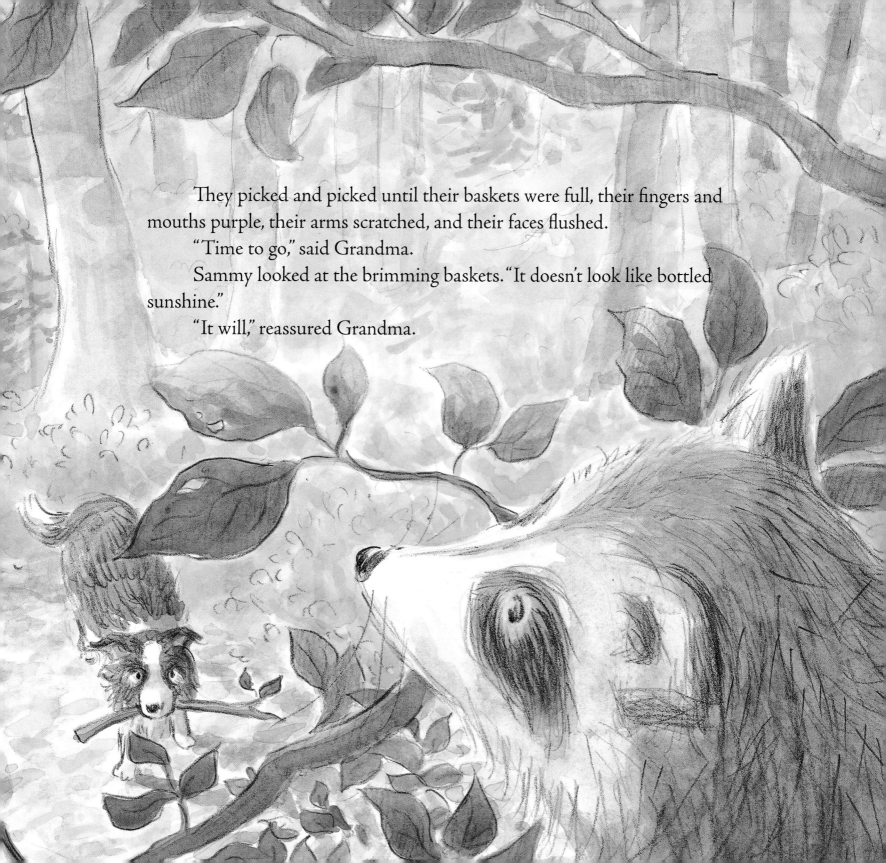

They picked and picked until their baskets were full, their fingers and mouths purple, their arms scratched, and their faces flushed.

"Time to go," said Grandma.

Sammy looked at the brimming baskets. "It doesn't look like bottled sunshine."

"It will," reassured Grandma.

They washed and drained the berries, measured them into a large pot, and added sugar.

Sammy, wrapped in Grandma's apron, stood on a stool. He helped stir the bubbling mess. "This REALLY doesn't look like sunshine."

"It will," said Grandma. "Be patient."

Grandma poured the jam into clean, shiny jars. Next she covered the top with a stream of hot, clear wax. It turned white as it cooled.

"What's that for?" asked Sammy.

"To seal in the sunshine and keep it fresh until it's needed," said Grandma.

By evening the kitchen table was full of jam. The setting sun streamed in through the window. The jars glowed.

The next day Sammy flew home. Packed safely in the middle of his bag was a large jar of bottled sunshine.

Sammy was pleased to see his room. He unpacked and looked around thoughtfully. Where was the safest place for his jar?

He walked over to his special shelf, moved a rock and his baseball mitt, and stood the bottled sunshine in the middle, right next to his pickled snake.

In September, school started and Sammy met his friends again. He joined computer club, signed up for his very own library card, and built a robot in the corner of the garage.

When the winter snows started, Sammy played hockey on the icy streets.

Christmas came and went. A racing car, a new computer game, and a glow-in-the-dark octopus were placed at the front of the special shelf.

The bottled sunshine gathered a layer of dust.

By February, winter became boring. It was too long, too cold, and too dark. It was dark when Sammy woke up. It was dark when he came home from school. The winter storms raged on and on, and everyone was snarly.

His mother was cross because he'd lost his third pair of mitts. His father was cross because the car wouldn't start. Sammy was cross because the batteries in his racing car were dead and the cat had eaten half of his glow-in-the-dark octopus.

The sun didn't shine for days.

One day the phone rang and his mother wept. Father told Sammy that Grandma had died.

Sammy ran to his bedroom and slammed the door hard. "I don't want Grandma to die!" he yelled

His mother lay beside him. She stroked Sammy's hair.

Sammy talked about Grandma— their days exploring the tide pools, the evening cuddles, the fishing trips, and the time they'd made jam.

He sat up, brushing his hands across his eyes. "I forgot."

Sammy slid off the bed and ran to his special shelf. The half-eaten octopus, baseball mitt, computer game, and racing car clattered to the floor. He lifted down the forgotten jar.

"We need bottled sunshine," he said.

Sammy carried the jar into the kitchen and wiped away the dust. The jar glowed.

He slipped a knife under the wax and lifted the seal. A smell of juicy summer blackberries stole into the kitchen.

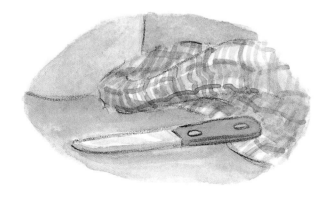

His mother sliced and buttered bread. Sammy took a piece, spread it with a thick layer of bottled sunshine, and tasted. His lips grew purple.

"I hear bees," exclaimed Sammy, "and feel prickles on my fingers. I can taste berries and feel the sun on my face."

His mother smiled.

He leaned over and offered her a bite.

The jam smudged her face. Sammy chuckled.

"Mom," he said, "you look just like a blackberry."